WAFFLE'S BIRTHDAY

Published in the UK by Scholastic Children's Books, 2020
Euston House, 24 Eversholt Street,
London NW1 1DB, UK
A division of Scholastic Limited

London ~ New York ~ Toronto ~ Sydney ~ Auckland
Mexico City ~ New Delhi ~ Hong Kong

DARRALL MACQUEEN LTD

TRADE ISBN 978 0702 30012 7
CLUBS AND FAIRS ISBN 978 0702 30072 1

A CIP catalogue record for this book is available from the British Library.

Printed and bound in Italy by L.E.G.O S.p.A

2 4 6 8 10 9 7 5 3 1

www.scholastic.co.uk

SCHOLASTIC

It was Waffle's first birthday with the Brooklyn-Bell family and Mr Willow had invited everyone round to his house for a party. There were balloons, bunting and even a bouncy castle.

"This is going to be a brilliant party!" smiled Evie.

"And it's all for YOU, Waffle!" said Jess.

"Woof!" barked Waffle happily.

"The birthday dog is here!" Mr Willow greeted Waffle. "Later on, we have a very special surprise for you!"

Everyone cheered and music began to play.

"Surprise! Surprise! Surprise, please!" woofed Waffle.

Gramps wagged his finger. "Be patient, Waffle. The surprise is for later."

"Awww!" whined Waffle.

Waffle decided he would go for a swim until it was time for his surprise. But the swimming pool was already busy – Mr Willow's dogs, Trevor and Violet, were splashing about and soaking all the party guests!

"Sorry, Waffle," said Mr Willow. "We don't want any more soggy doggies."

The bouncy castle looked fun. "Waffle, bounce?" asked Waffle, wagging his tail.

"Ah, no," Mr Willow said again. "Bouncy castles aren't for dogs."

"Humph," woofed Waffle.

Then Waffle had a tasty idea. "Waffle, food?" he said, licking his lips.

"No, Waffle!" smiled Mr Willow. "We won't be eating the party food until all of the guests have arrived."

Waffle frowned. Everyone was having fun except him! "Go play with your friends, Waffle," said Gramps kindly.

So Waffle went to find his friend George the cat.

"Not fair, Georgey," Waffle moaned. "Waffle swim – no! Waffle bounce – no!"

George snuggled down into his cushion and began to purr ... then he began to snore!

"Georgey?" woofed Waffle. "Oh, no!"

The kitty had fallen fast asleep. *Zzzz!*

Just then, Connie and Ruby arrived with their dog, Jelly ... Waffle's fun was about to begin!

"Jelly says 'Happy Birthday'!" said Ruby. "Thanks for inviting her."

Suddenly, Jelly had spotted something exciting and ran straight past Waffle.

"Jelly, come back!" called Waffle, as Jelly jumped on to the bouncy castle.

"Hey! No dogs allowed!" said the bouncy castle man. He tried to catch Jelly but ended up falling on his bottom!

Next, Jelly raced to the swimming pool.

"Jelly," called Waffle. "Stop!"

But Jelly wasn't listening. She jumped into the pool with a great big splash and began doggy-paddling. It looked like so much fun that Waffle jumped in too! *Splash*!

After a quick swim, the two dogs got out and shook themselves dry, spraying Mrs Hobbs with water!

"Waffle! You know what Mr Willow said — no swimming," Gramps warned.

"Sorry," said Waffle sadly.

Meanwhile, Jess, Simon and the children were getting Waffle's special surprise ready. Everyone was helping to carry a big stage to the other side of the garden.

"Quick!" said Jess. "Waffle's coming, he'll see!"

Waffle wandered up to take a look. "What is that?" he woofed.

"Nothing!" said Evie.
"Go and play with Jelly, Waffle," said Jess, shooing him away.
So, Waffle went to find his doggie friend.

Waffle spotted Jelly, disappearing into the tent with all the party food. Inside, Jelly was already helping herself to a plate of sausages!

"Mmm!" said Waffle when he saw the yummy food. "My turn!" He jumped on to the table and began munching on crisps and cakes. *Crunch*! *Chomp*!

Outside, Doug got up on stage. "As everyone knows, Waffle is a really good dog," said Doug, over the microphone. "So here is his surprise..."

When Waffle heard Doug, he felt guilty ... he knew that eating all the party food was not something a good dog would do!

Waffle's surprise was a song that the Brooklyn-Bell family had written especially for Waffle!

"Waffle makes us happy every day, and we're glad that he wants to stay..." the family began to sing.

But Waffle was nowhere to be seen. "Where are you, Waffle?" called Doug.

Inside the tent, Waffle's ears pricked up when he heard Doug call his name.

"My surprise!" woofed Waffle. "Sorry, Jelly! I've got to go!"

But Jelly raced out of the tent first, tripping over the rope that was holding it up. Suddenly, the tent tumbled to the floor. What a mess! Now Waffle was really in trouble...

Everyone was very quiet for a moment, and then Mr Willow began to laugh. "It's okay, Waffle," he said. "It's your party!"

"Silly pup!" smiled Jess. "We were so busy with your surprise, it's no wonder you got up to mischief!"

Soon, it was time for another song. This time, Waffle was the star. He started to sing,

"Oh Waffle, I'm Waffle, leaping around like a frog!
I just want to say one thing: I'm such a clever dog!"

And then everyone joined in!
"Waffle doggy! Waffle doggy!
You're such a clever dog,
You're such a clever dog, you are..."

When the song had finished, Jess took a family selfie to remember the special day. "Everyone say, 'dog biscuits!'" she smiled.

"Woof!" barked Waffle happily. "Best. Party. Ever!"